stuffed

emma bray

Copyright © 2024 by Emma Bray

All rights reserved.

No part of this book may be reproduced in any form or by any electronic or mechanical means, including information storage and retrieval systems, without written permission from the author, except for the use of brief quotations in a book review.

one

. . .

Claire

THE AROMA of freshly baked pumpkin bread wafts through my cozy apartment as I snap the perfect photo for my latest blog post. Golden light streams through the lace curtains, casting an ethereal glow across the rustic wooden table. I smile to myself, imagining the delighted reactions from my followers once they see this tantalizing image.

Just as I upload the picture, my phone buzzes insistently. It's my mother. I pause, then swipe to answer. "Hello?"

"Claire, darling! I have exciting news," she chirps, her voice brimming with barely contained enthusiasm. "Thanksgiving dinner this year will be at the Rosewood Inn. You remember, the charming place just outside of town?"

I twirl a auburn curl around my finger, trying to recall the inn. Vague memories of a quaint, ivy-covered building nestled among crimson maples surface in my mind.

"Oh right, I think I know the one," I reply, my brow furrowing slightly. "But why there? I thought Aunt Lily always hosted."

"Well, that's the thing," Mom continues, her tone turning conspiratorial. "The inn was recently taken over by a rather dashing young chef named Jax. Apparently he's causing quite the stir with his innovative Thanksgiving menu. And I was thinking…maybe a little collaboration with him would be great for your brand."

A tingle of curiosity mixed with anticipation dances down my spine at the mention of this mysterious newcomer. I glance at the array of glossy cookbooks lining my shelves, their spines whispering of mouthwatering possibilities.

"A new chef in town? Color me intrigued," I say, absently running my fingers along the embossed lettering of a well-worn Julia Child tome. The prospect of sampling some inventive holiday dishes sends a thrill through me.

"I thought you would be, dear. You simply must meet him! The way he's reinventing traditional recipes is right up your alley."

My mind is already spinning, conjuring up blog post titles and imagining the stunning food photography I could capture at the inn. This Jax fellow might be just the inspiration I need to kick my culinary content up a notch.

"Alright Mom, you've piqued my interest. Send me the details," I say with a smile, already mentally planning my outfit and eyeing my trusty DSLR camera.

As we say our goodbyes, I turn back to the bread cooling on the rack, its warm spices perfuming the air with the essence of fall.

The gravel crunches beneath my boots as I step out of the car, inhaling deeply. The air is laced with the earthy scent of fallen leaves and distant wood smoke, a sensory reminder that the holiday season is fast approaching. I smooth my hands over the rich burgundy fabric of my sweater dress, hoping it strikes the right balance between professional and alluring.

Stepping through the inn's heavy wooden door,

I'm immediately enveloped by the warm glow of the foyer. Antique furnishings and the soft crackle of a fireplace create an inviting ambiance that speaks to the building's rich history. As I take in the charming details, my mother's voice pulls me from my reverie.

"Claire! You made it," she trills, sweeping me into a hug that smells faintly of her signature Chanel perfume. "Come, let me introduce you to Jax. He's been eager to meet the talented daughter I've been bragging about."

I follow her through the cozy sitting room, my heels sinking into the plush Oriental rug. Anticipation hums through my veins as we approach the kitchen, the muffled clang of pots and pans hinting at the culinary magic within.

And then, there he is.

Jax Donovan looks up from his workstation, a roguish grin playing at the corners of his mouth. Holy fuck, my mom never mentioned how *hot* he is. The man looks like he belongs on the cover of a magazine, with tousled dark hair and eyes that sparkle with mischief. The sleeves of his crisp white chef's jacket are rolled up, revealing tanned forearms dusted with fine dark hair.

"Ah, the renowned food blogger graces us with her presence," he says, wiping his hands on a towel before extending one in greeting. His handshake is firm and warm, sending a jolt of electricity up my arm.

"Chef Donovan," I reply, hoping my voice doesn't betray the butterflies suddenly taking flight in my stomach. "I've heard great things about your culinary prowess. I'm looking forward to seeing what you have in store for Thanksgiving."

His eyes lock with mine, a flicker of heat passing between us. "Please, call me Jax. And I assure you, Ms. Harper, my kitchen is your playground. I have a feeling we're going to create some magic together."

The air feels charged, heavy with unspoken promises and the tantalizing scent of simmering spices. I feel my cheeks heating and mentally curse myself.

Damn my propensity for blushing.

My mother, apparently oblivious, chirps cheerily, "Well, I'll leave you two to it. Claire, I'll see you later, darling!"

I don't even know if I tell my mom goodbye. I can't break the pull of Jax's stare that has me held captive.

I swallow and nervously tuck a stray curl behind my ear, Jax watching my every movement like a hawk. I watch the way his eyes rove over me from head to toe. Maybe I should be offended by the lazy way he's perusing me, but I'm not.

I'm flattered—and flustered.

Jax studies me a moment longer before he smiles a panty-dropping smile and guides me through the bustling kitchen, his hand resting lightly on the small of my back. The heat of his touch seeps through the thin fabric of my blouse, igniting a slow burn beneath my skin. He introduces me to his staff, a well-oiled machine of sous chefs and prep cooks, each focused intently on their tasks.

"So, Claire," Jax says, turning to face me with a playful glint in his eye. "I hear you've got some strong opinions about the perfect Thanksgiving menu."

I arch a brow, meeting his gaze head-on. "I believe in honoring tradition while elevating the classics. It's all about striking the right balance."

He leans in closer, his breath warm against my ear. "And let me guess, you like to be in control of every little detail?"

I feel a flush creeping up my neck, but I refuse to back down. "I prefer to think of it as having a vision and executing it flawlessly."

Jax chuckles, the sound low and intimate. "Well, I hope you're ready to relinquish a little of that control, Claire. Because in my kitchen, we play by my rules."

The way my name rolls off his tongue sends a shiver down my spine. There's a challenge in his words, a promise of something thrilling and unknown. I find myself leaning into him, drawn by an inexplicable force.

"And what exactly are your rules, Chef Donovan?" I ask, my voice barely above a whisper.

His eyes darken, the air between us electric with tension. "Rule number one: trust your instincts. Rule number two: take risks. And rule number three..." He pauses, his gaze dropping to my lips. "Always save room for dessert."

My heart hammers against my ribcage, the implication of his words causing heat to pool low in my belly. Jax steps back, the moment broken but the intensity still simmering beneath the surface.

"Now, let's talk turkey," he says with a wink, gesturing to the prep station behind him. "I've got some ideas that will make your taste buds sing."

As we dive into the Thanksgiving menu planning, Jax's enthusiasm is infectious. He moves around the kitchen with a fluid grace, his hands gesturing animatedly as he describes his vision for each dish. I find myself drawn into his world, captivated by the passion that radiates from him.

"I've been experimenting with a new stuffing recipe," Jax says, his eyes sparkling with excitement. "It's a twist on the classic, with chestnuts, pancetta, and a hint of sage."

He reaches for a bowl of the fragrant mixture, holding it out for me to sample. I lean in, inhaling the heady aroma of toasted bread and savory herbs. Jax watches me intently, a small smile playing at the corners of his mouth.

"May I?" I ask, my fingers hovering over the bowl.

"Be my guest," he replies, his voice low and inviting.

I pluck a morsel from the bowl and bring it to my lips, my eyes fluttering closed as the flavors explode on my tongue. The stuffing is a perfect balance of texture and taste, the chestnuts providing a subtle sweetness that complements the salty pancetta and earthy sage.

"Jax, this is incredible," I breathe, my eyes opening to meet his gaze.

He leans in closer, his breath warm against my cheek. "I'm glad you approve. I put a lot of thought into the...stuffing."

The way he says "stuffing," with a slight pause and a mischievous glint in his eye, sends a rush of heat through my body. I feel my cheeks flush, and

I know it has nothing to do with the warm kitchen.

Jax's smile widens, clearly enjoying the effect he has on me. "I hope you'll like my stuffing as much as I enjoy making it for you, Claire."

His words are laced with innuendo, the double entendre hanging heavily in the air between us. I swallow hard, my mind conjuring up images that have no place in a professional kitchen.

"I have no doubt that I will," I manage to reply, my voice sounding breathy even to my own ears.

Jax holds my gaze a moment longer, the tension crackling like electricity. Then, with a wink, he turns back to the stove, leaving me to compose myself.

As we continue to work side by side, sampling dishes and exchanging ideas, I can't help but be hyperaware of Jax's presence. Every brush of his arm against mine, every lingering glance, sends a thrill through me. The kitchen seems to shrink, the space between us charged with unspoken desire.

The aromas of cinnamon, cloves, and roasting turkey mingle in the air, creating a heady perfume that only adds to the intoxicating atmosphere. Jax moves with a sensual confidence, his hands deftly chopping, stirring, and seasoning each dish with expert precision, Jax is in his element in the kitchen.

I find myself captivated by his every move, the way his muscles flex beneath his chef's jacket as he works. He catches me staring and flashes me a knowing grin, his eyes glinting with mischief.

"See something you like, Claire?" he teases, his voice low and husky.

I feel the heat rising in my cheeks, but I refuse to look away. "Maybe I do," I reply, my own voice taking on a flirtatious edge.

Jax chuckles, the sound sending a shiver down my spine.

His words hang in the air, the implication clear. I feel a thrill of excitement mixed with nerves. This is dangerous territory, flirting with a man I barely know in his own kitchen. But there's something about Jax that draws me in, makes me want to throw caution to the wind.

We continue to work, the tension simmering between us like a pot ready to boil over. Every accidental touch, every heated glance, only serves to stoke the flames of desire. I find myself getting lost in the rhythmic chopping of vegetables, the sizzle of meat in a hot pan, the dance of flavors as Jax expertly crafts each dish.

As the day wears on and the menu takes shape, I realize that I've never felt so inspired, so alive, in my entire culinary career. Jax's passion for food is contagious, his innovative ideas sparking my own creativity. We bounce ideas off each other, our excitement growing with each new twist on a classic recipe.

"I have to say, Claire," Jax murmurs as we stand side by side, surveying the fruits of our labor. "You're even more impressive in person than you are on your blog. I could get used to having you around my kitchen."

I glance up at him through my lashes, my heart skipping a beat at the heat in his gaze. "Is that so? Well, maybe we should make this a regular thing. For the sake of our culinary growth, of course."

"Of course," he agrees, a slow smile spreading across his face. "Purely professional."

But the way his eyes rake over my body, the way his hand lingers on the small of my back as he guides me to the sink to wash up, tells a different story. I can feel the promise of something more, the tantalizing possibility of exploring this connection between us beyond the confines of the kitchen.

As we say our goodbyes, Jax's fingers brush against mine, sending a jolt of electricity through me. "Until next time, Claire," he murmurs, his voice a caress. "I look forward to tasting more."

Of you. It hangs in the air between us even though he doesn't complete the sentence.

I swallow hard, my mouth suddenly dry.

I don't speak. Hell, I can't.

With one last smoldering look, he steps back, allowing me to exit the kitchen on slightly unsteady legs. As I make my way out of the inn, I can still feel the ghost of his touch on my skin, the heat of his gaze burning into my memory.

Good lord, what have I gotten myself into?

two
. . .

Jax

I CLOSE the door behind Claire, her floral scent still lingering in the air. My pulse races as I picture her captivating eyes, the curve of her lips as she smiled at me. I lean back against the door, desire coursing through my veins. I can't stop thinking about her—the way she moved with such confidence in the kitchen, the passion in her voice as she spoke about flavors and techniques. My body responds to the mere thought of her.

I make my way to the bedroom, images of Claire dancing through my mind. Settling onto the bed, I recall the first time I saw her. It was one of her blog videos, where she was demonstrating a decadent chocolate soufflé. I was transfixed by her charisma, the way she commanded the screen. I must have watched that video a dozen times, studying every nuance of her expressions, every graceful gesture of her hands.

My fingers tremble slightly as I unbutton my jeans, freeing my hardened cock. I wrap my hand around the shaft, stroking slowly as I lose myself in fantasies of Claire. I imagine her here with me, her soft skin pressed against mine, her breath hot against my neck. I picture her hands exploring my body, teasing and arousing me until I'm aching for her touch.

The truth is, she's the reason I uprooted my life and moved to this small town. When I learned my uncle had left me the inn, it felt like fate—a chance to finally meet Claire in person, to find a way into her world. Some might call it obsession, the way I've followed her career, the way I've dreamed of her late at night. But to me, it's an irresistible pull, a need to know her, to unravel the mysteries that lie beneath her vibrant surface.

My hand moves faster now, urgency building as I lose myself in the fantasy. I imagine tasting her, savoring her essence like a gourmet meal. I picture her writhing beneath me, her lips parted in ecstasy as I bring her to the brink of pleasure again and again. The bed creaks softly as my hips rock in rhythm with my strokes, chasing the release that hovers just out of reach.

Claire's name falls from my lips like a prayer as I reach my climax, spilling over my fist with a shuddering groan. For a moment, I simply lie there, chest heaving, lost in the afterglow of my desire. But even as the physical urgency fades, the longing remains—a hunger that can only be sated by the real thing. One way or another, I vow to myself, I'll find a way to make Claire mine.

No matter what it takes.

The next day, I wake early, the memory of my steamy dreams still lingering in the back of my mind.

Claire laying underneath, her hair splayed out around her as I claimed her as mine...

The taste of her pussy...

The way her eyes looked up at me as she had my cock between her swollen lips...

My cock is rock hard, but I ignore it. Instead, I shower and dress, my movements efficient but preoccupied. She's coming over again today, and I can hardly wait.

My cock is leaking just thinking about it. The fucking girl has me in a current state of arousal.

I'm in the kitchen when I hear the sound of her heels clacking confidently down the hallway. My heartbeat quickens as I picture her, a vision in her trademark apron, hair falling in loose waves around her flushed face. The kitchen door swings open, and there she is, every bit as breathtaking as always. "Morning, Jax," she greets me prettily. "What tricks have you got up your sleeve today?"

"Oh, I've got a few tricks up my sleeve," I say, allowing my voice to drop into a lower register. We share a charged moment, both of us aware of the electricity crackling between us. "But first," I add, clearing my throat, "I thought we could start with a Thanksgiving classic. Turkey and stuffing."

"Now that's my kind of language," she teases, and we both laugh, the tension temporarily dispersed. We set to work side by side, the scents of pine and cinnamon swirling around us as we begin preparing the feast. Despite the growing heat in the kitchen, I find myself drawn to her like a moth to flame.

As we work, I make a point of brushing past her "accidentally," my body thrumming with awareness each time our skin touches. I catch her glancing at me through lowered lashes, and I know she feels it too. The chemistry between us is undeniable, as potent as the aromas wafting through the air.

And I dare to hope that this beautiful creature wants me too.

As the morning sun filters through the windows, casting dappled shadows on her face, I can't help but recall the countless nights I've spent watching her online, fantasizing about this very moment. I've imagined every curve of her body, every breathy moan she'd utter as I taste my way across her skin. It's all I've thought about since I saw her for the first time, cooking up that decadent concoction with a flirty smile and a twinkle in her eye.

I'd known then and there, with a bone-deep certainty, that I needed her in my life. And now, here she is, standing just inches away from me, her delicious scent mingling with the mouthwatering fragrances of our Thanksgiving feast.

As we work side by side, chopping vegetables and prepping ingredients, I find myself drawn into conversation with Claire, eager to learn more about her life and passions. "So, what brings you to our little corner of the world?" she asks, her eyes bright with curiosity. "I heard you inherited the inn from your uncle?"

I nod, a wistful smile tugging at my lips. "Yeah, it was unexpected. He passed away a few months ago, and I found out he'd left me this place in his will. It felt like a sign, you know? A chance to start fresh, to build something of my own."

Claire's expression softens with sympathy. "I'm sorry for your loss," she says gently. "It must have been a big decision, leaving your old life behind like that."

"It was," I agree, my gaze drifting to the window, where the autumn leaves dance in the breeze. "But sometimes, you just know when it's time for a change. When an opportunity presents itself, you have to grab it with both hands."

My words hang in the air between us, heavy with unspoken meaning. I can feel Claire's eyes on me, searching my face for clues to the secrets I'm not yet ready to reveal. The truth is, my uncle's death was just the catalyst I needed to finally pursue my obsession with her. But I can't tell her that, not yet. Not when I've just begun to earn her trust.

Instead, I steer the conversation back to safer ground, regaling her with tales of my culinary adventures in the city. She listens intently, her laughter ringing out like music as I describe some of my more disastrous experiments in the kitchen. All the while, I'm acutely aware of her presence beside me, the heat of her body, the brush of her arm against mine as we work.

As the morning wears on, the tension between us grows, simmering like a pot on the verge of boiling over. Every accidental touch, every lingering glance feels charged with electricity, until the air practically crackles with it. And when Claire reaches across me for a spice jar, her fingers grazing my hand, I can't help but let out a soft hiss of breath.

She glances up at me through her lashes, her cheeks flushed pink. "Sorry," she murmurs, but I can tell by the gleam in her eye that she's not sorry at all.

"No problem," I manage, my voice rougher than usual. "I'm just excited to get this turkey stuffed. Among other things."

The words slip out before I can stop them, laced with innuendo. Claire's eyes widen, and she bites her lip, her cheeks flushing an even deeper shade of pink at my bold innuendo. She tries to play it cool, busying herself with the stuffing mixture, but I can see the effect my words have had on her. The air between us is thick with tension, crackling with unspoken desire.

I step closer, crowding into her personal space until I can feel the heat radiating off her body. She keeps her eyes downcast, focused intently on her task, but her hands tremble slightly as she works. I reach out, my fingers grazing the delicate skin of her wrist, and she sucks in a sharp breath.

"Careful," I murmur, my voice low and intimate. "Wouldn't want you to hurt yourself."

Claire swallows hard, finally meeting my gaze. Her eyes are dark, pupils blown wide with arousal. "I can handle myself just fine," she says, but her voice wavers slightly.

I lean in even closer until my lips are just a hairsbreadth from her ear. "Oh, I have no doubt about that," I breathe. "But sometimes it's more fun to let someone else take the reins, don't you think?"

She shivers, her eyes fluttering closed for a brief moment. When she opens them again, there's a new intensity burning in their depths. "Is that what you want, Jax?" she asks, her voice husky. "To take the reins?"

I let my gaze travel slowly down her body, taking in every lush curve, every tantalizing inch of her. "Oh, sweetheart," I drawl. "You have no idea what I want to do to you."

Fuck, it's all I can do to hold back. My cock is dripping precum in my pants, and I'm surprised she hasn't noticed the obscene tent it's making yet.

Claire's breath hitches, her lips parting slightly. I can practically taste her desire, sweet and heady on my tongue. It takes every ounce of willpower I possess not to close the distance between us, to claim her mouth with my own and lose myself in her intoxicating kiss.

But I force myself to hold back, to savor the delicious tension building between us. I want to draw this out, to tease and tantalize her until she's trembling with need, until she's begging me for more.

Until there's absolutely no way she'll deny me.

My cock throbs insistently against the confines of my jeans, hard as steel and aching for her touch. I shift slightly, trying to ease the pressure, but it's no use. Every movement, every brush of fabric against my sensitive skin only serves to heighten my arousal.

Claire's gaze flickers downward, her eyes widening slightly as she takes in the prominent bulge at the front of my pants. Her tongue darts out to wet her lips, a seemingly unconscious gesture that sends a bolt of pure lust straight to my groin.

She blushes furiously, tearing her gaze away

from my crotch. "I...we should get..." she trips over her words and trails off.

I lean in closer, my lips grazing the shell of her ear. "What's the matter, Claire?" I murmur, my voice a low rumble. "Feeling a little flustered?"

She shivers, her breath coming faster now. "I...we have a lot of work to do," she manages, but her voice lacks conviction.

"Mmm, that we do," I agree, letting my fingers trail lightly up her arm. "But I think we can spare a moment, don't you?"

Claire's eyes flutter closed as my touch ignites sparks across her skin. "Jax..." she breathes, my name a plea and a warning all at once.

I nuzzle into the crook of her neck, inhaling deeply. She smells like cinnamon and desire, an intoxicating combination that makes my head spin. Fuck, I'm drowning. "God, you're irresistible," I groan, pressing a hot, open-mouthed kiss to her racing pulse. "I bet you're sweet as maple syrup aren't you, sugar?"

A soft whimper escapes her, and I feel her melting into me, her resistance crumbling under the onslaught of sensation. Emboldened, I let my hands roam her curves, mapping the dips and swells of her body through the thin fabric of her dress.

Claire arches into my touch, a breathy moan falling from her lips as I cup her breast, kneading the soft flesh. Her nipple pebbles against my palm, and I can't resist giving it a light pinch, relishing the way she jerks and gasps in response.

"You like that, sweetheart?" I rasp, my voice rough with need. "You like it when I touch you?"

"Yes," she hisses, grinding her hips against me, seeking friction. "God, yes."

I capture her mouth in a searing kiss, swallowing her moans as our tongues tangle and dance. She tastes like heaven, sweet and addictive, and I know I'll never get enough. My hands find the hem of her skirt, slipping beneath to stroke the silky skin of her thighs.

Claire's hands fist in my hair, holding me to her as she kisses me back with abandon. I can feel the heat of her through her thin panties, and it takes every ounce of willpower not to rip them away and bury myself inside her right here in the kitchen.

But I want to savor this, to take my time worshipping every inch of her until she's writhing and desperate, until she forgets her own name. Reluctantly, I break the kiss, my breathing ragged as I rest my forehead against hers.

"Later," I promise, my voice a dark whisper full of sinful intent. "After dinner, I'm going to spread you out on my bed and feast on you until you scream."

Claire shudders, her eyes glazed with lust as she stares up at me. "

Claire shudders, her eyes glazed with lust as she stares up at me. "Promises, promises," she murmurs breathlessly, a coy smile playing at the corners of her kiss-swollen lips.

I chuckle, low and dark, my fingers still teasing the sensitive skin of her inner thighs. "Oh, I always keep my promises, sweetheart. You'll see."

With a supreme effort of will, I force myself to step back, putting a modicum of distance between us before I lose control entirely and take her right here against the kitchen counter. My cock throbs painfully, straining against my zipper, but I ignore it.

There will be time enough for that later. For now, I intend to revel in the delicious anticipation, to let the tension build until it's a living, breathing thing between us.

Claire takes a shaky breath, smoothing her hands over her skirt in a futile attempt to compose herself. "We should...we should get back to work," she says, but her voice lacks conviction.

"Mmm, I suppose we should," I agree, though I make no move to do so. Instead, I let my gaze travel over her leisurely, drinking in the sight of her flushed cheeks, her heaving chest, the way her nipples press against the thin fabric of her blouse. "Wouldn't want to leave our guests unsatisfied, now would we?"

The double entendre hangs heavy in the air between us, and Claire's breath hitches. "No," she says softly, her eyes locked on mine. "No, we wouldn't want that."

Slowly, deliberately, I reach out and trail a finger along the delicate line of her collarbone, relishing the way she shivers at my touch. "Then let's get to it," I murmur, my voice a velvet caress. "We've got a feast to prepare."

And oh, what a feast it will be. The thought of finally tasting her, of burying myself in her sweet heat and feeling her come undone around me, is almost more than I can bear. But I am a patient man, and I know that the wait will only make the eventual payoff that much sweeter.

For now, I content myself with stolen glances and fleeting touches as we work side by side, our bodies brushing tantalizingly as we move around the kitchen. Every accidental caress, every heated look, only serves to stoke the flames of my desire, until I'm practically vibrating with the need to claim her.

By the time the turkey is in the oven and the side dishes are prepped, I'm wound tighter than a bowstring, my control fraying at the edges. Claire seems to sense it, her own movements growing more languid, more deliberately provocative as the day wears on.

As she reaches up to grab a spice from the top shelf, her blouse rides up to reveal a tantalizing strip of skin at her waist.

My throat goes dry.

Claire's blouse inches up higher as she stretches for the spice jar, exposing the smooth expanse of her lower back. My breath catches at the tantalizing glimpse of bare skin. Without thinking, I step up behind her, my chest pressing against her back as I easily reach the jar she was straining for.

"Here, let me help with that," I murmur, my lips grazing her ear. She shivers, a soft gasp escaping her parted lips as she leans back into me. I set the spice aside, my hands coming to rest on her hips, fingers teasing along the waistband of her skirt.

"Jax..." she breathes, half warning, half plea. I nuzzle into the crook of her neck, drinking in her intoxicating scent.

"You smell incredible," I rasp, pressing hot, open-mouthed kisses along the column of her throat. "Good enough to eat."

Claire whimpers, tilting her head to give me better access even as she weakly protests. "We can't...the turkey..."

I chuckle darkly, nipping at her earlobe. "Fuck the turkey. I'd rather stuff you instead."

She shudders, a needy moan spilling from her lips as she rocks back against me. I'm painfully hard, my cock throbbing insistently against the curve of her ass. Sliding my hands up her sides, I cup her breasts, kneading the soft mounds through the thin fabric of her blouse.

"You feel what you do to me?" I growl, grinding against her. "How fucking hard you make me? I've been half out of my mind wanting you."

Claire arches into my touch, her head falling back onto my shoulder. "Jax, please..."

I turn her in my arms and claim her mouth in a searing kiss, hot and hungry and full of pent up desire. She opens for me beautifully, her tongue tangling with mine as I walk her backwards until she hits the counter. Hoisting her up, I step between her parted thighs, my hands pushing her skirt up around her hips.

She wraps her legs around my waist, heels digging into my ass as she pulls me closer. I can feel her heat through the damp lace of her panties, and it takes every ounce of restraint not to rip them off and bury myself inside her right here.

But I want to savor this, to take my time worshipping her until she's mindless with pleasure. Trailing my lips down the elegant column of her neck, I leave a path of hot, open-mouthed kisses across her collarbone as my fingers work the buttons of her blouse.

Claire's hands fist in my hair, holding me to her as she arches into my touch. Popping the last button, I push the fabric aside, groaning at the sight of her luscious curves encased in delicate white lace. "Fuck, you're stunning," I breathe reverently, tracing a finger along the scalloped edge of her bra.

Claire flushes prettily under my heated gaze. "Touch me, Jax," she pleads, her voice breathy with need. "I want your hands on me."

I'm only too happy to oblige. Reaching behind her, I deftly unhook the clasp, freeing her breasts from their lacy confines. They spill into my waiting hands, soft and supple, the rosy peaks already puckered and begging for attention.

Lowering my head, I capture one aching nipple between my lips, swirling my tongue around the sensitive bud. Claire cries out, her back bowing as she fists her hands in my hair. I lavish her with attention, suckling and nipping until she's writhing against me, desperate for more.

My other hand skates down her trembling stomach to slip beneath the waistband of her panties. She's dripping wet, her slick folds parting easily as I tease along her slit. "Always so ready for me," I groan against her breast. "So fucking responsive."

"Please," she whimpers, hips canting shamelessly into my touch.

I circle her clit with the pad of my thumb, relishing her sharp intake of breath. Slowly, torturously, I ease one long finger inside her, then two, pumping in a steady rhythm that has her mewling and panting my name like a prayer.

And then I feel the barrier of her hymen, and I swear I jizz a little in my pants when the realization hits me.

A virgin. *Mine.* All mine. Claire will only ever belong to *me.*

She's tight and scorching hot around my fingers, her inner walls fluttering wildly as I bring her closer and closer to the edge, careful not to break the barrier of her virginity. No, I'm doing that with my cock.

I keep gently fucking her with my fingers, though. I can tell she's close by the desperate pitch of her cries, the erratic buck and roll of her hips against my hand.

"That's it, baby," I coax hotly, curling my fingers to stroke that secret spot deep inside her. "Let go for me. I want to feel you come all over my hand."

Claire shatters with a sobbing cry, her head thrown back in ecstasy as wave after wave of pleasure crashes over her. I work her through it, prolonging her bliss until she's boneless and trembling in my arms.

Slowly, reluctantly, I ease my fingers from her still quivering body, bringing them to my lips to savor her essence. She watches me through heavy-lidded eyes, her chest heaving as she tries to catch her breath.

"You taste divine," I tell her, my voice ragged with desire. "But I'm not nearly done feasting on you yet."

Her eyes widen as I sink to my knees before her, hooking my fingers in her ruined panties and dragging them down her shapely legs. Tossing them aside, I nudge her thighs further apart, exposing her beautiful folds.

I pause, gazing at Claire's glistening pussy, savoring the sight of her spread open before me. She's perfect, pink and swollen and dripping with arousal. My mouth waters with the need to taste her.

"Jax..." Claire whimpers, her voice thick with need. "Please..."

I smirk up at her. "Please what, sweetheart? Tell me what you want."

She flushes, biting her plump lower lip. "I want...I don't know, but I need..."

Fuck, hearing her beg for it nearly undoes me. I lean in, inhaling her intoxicating scent. "I know what you need, baby," I murmur, before swiping my tongue along her slick folds.

Claire bucks, crying out at the first intimate touch. I grip her hips, holding her steady as I set to work, laving her sensitive flesh with long, slow licks. She tastes exquisite, tangy and sweet, and I groan against her, the vibrations making her tremble.

I take my time, exploring every inch of her, teasing out each breathy moan and desperate whimper. Claire's hands fist in my hair as I circle her clit with the tip of my tongue, flicking the swollen bud until she's writhing mindlessly.

"Oh god, Jax, yes! Right there, don't stop!" she pants, grinding against my face. I seal my lips around her clit and suckle hard, plunging two fingers deep into her tight channel.

Claire unravels with a keening wail, her virgin pussy clenching rhythmically around my fingers as the orgasm tears through her. I lap at her greedily, prolonging her ecstasy, until she sags back against the counter, utterly spent.

Slowly, I rise to my feet, licking her essence from my lips. Claire watches me with hooded eyes, her chest heaving. I lean in, claiming her mouth in a filthy kiss, letting her taste herself on my tongue.

She moans into the kiss, clutching at my shoulders. I'm painfully hard, my cock straining insistently against my zipper, but I force myself to pull back. I want her in my bed for what comes next.

And then the fucking timer goes off on the oven.

three

. . .

Claire

THE KITCHEN TIMER sounds with a loud buzz, jolting me from the dreamy haze of peeling potatoes side by side with Jax. He mutters a curse under his breath.

"Hang on," he says, quickly adjusting the oven dials. He turns back to me, his eyes smoldering at me like melted chocolate. "Let's put this on warm for now."

My heart flutters as he takes my hand, his skin warm and slightly rough against mine. He leads me out of the kitchen and up a narrow wooden staircase, the old steps creaking beneath our feet.

With each step, the tension between us builds, electric and palpable, sending shivers racing along my spine.

At the top of the stairs, Jax guides me down a dimly lit hallway to a door at the very end. He produces an old brass key, unlocking the door and gesturing for me to enter. Intrigued, I step inside.

It's his private quarters—a cozy space with sloped ceilings, exposed wooden beams, and a large bed draped in a patchwork quilt. The room is lit only by the soft glow of an antique lamp on the nightstand. The air feels charged, crackling with unspoken desire.

The moment the door clicks shut behind us, Jax turns to me. In one fluid motion, he gently presses me back against the door, one hand cupping my cheek, the other snaking around my waist to draw me close. I catch my breath, pulse hammering in my ears.

"Claire," he murmurs, his lips a hair's breadth from mine. "Tell me you want this too."

In answer, I wind my arms around his neck and pull him down into a searing kiss. His mouth claims mine, hot and hungry, tasting of cinnamon and longing. I pour everything I feel into the kiss—the days of flirting, the aching want, the need flaring bright between us. He groans softly and deepens the kiss, his tongue sliding against mine, igniting sparks behind my closed eyelids.

Every inch of me burns for his touch. I've never wanted anyone like this, with an intensity that borders on desperation. All coherent thought flees my mind as his lips trail fire along my jaw, down the column of my throat.

This is a point of no return. Standing here in Jax's arms, lost in his passionate embrace, I know there will be no going back. Wherever this leads, whatever the consequences, I'm his—mind, body and soul. The realization is terrifying and thrilling all at once.

Jax's talented fingers slowly unzip my dress, each tooth releasing with a soft purr that seems to echo the pounding of my heart. Cool air kisses my overheated skin as the silky fabric parts and pools at my feet. I'm left standing in nothing but my lace bra and panties, shivering under the intensity of his molten gaze.

"God, you're exquisite," he whispers reverently, calloused hands skimming my sides, igniting trails of goosebumps in their wake. "A work of art."

Self-consciousness wars with arousal as I fight the urge to cover myself. But the raw hunger in Jax's eyes chases away any lingering doubts. He looks at me like a man starved, like I'm the most desirable thing he's ever seen.

Emboldened, I reach out to unbutton his shirt, my fingers trembling slightly as I reveal the hard planes of his chest, the roped muscle of his abs. He is strength and power, barely leashed. The air thickens, charged with an electric current of anticipation.

Jax walks me backward until my legs hit the edge of the bed. He lowers me down gently, covering my body with his own, a delicious weight that sets every nerve ending alight. I've never been this close to a man before, skin to skin, heartbeat to drumming heartbeat.

"I'm going to worship every inch of you," Jax promises darkly, his breath hot against my ear. "Until you're begging for release. Until my name is the only word you remember."

He captures my wrists and raises them above my head, pressing them into the pillows in a wordless command to keep them there. I obey instinctively, my body his willing canvas to paint with pleasure.

Then his mouth is everywhere—mapping the curve of my breast, the dip of my navel, the sensitive skin of my inner thigh. He uses lips and tongue and teeth to stoke the fire burning through my veins, higher and hotter, until I'm writhing beneath him, wordless pleas falling from my lips.

No fantasy could have prepared me for the reality of Jax's touch, at once torturously tender and fiercely possessive. He teases and tempts, stoking my arousal to a fever pitch, until I'm teetering on a knife's edge of excruciating bliss.

"Say it," he demands, his voice gruff and rasping against my skin. "Tell me what you want."

"I...I want...more," I gasp out, barely recognizing the needy moan issuing from my own lips.

He chuckles, deep and low, the vibration of his laughter sending fresh shivers through me. "I thought you might say that."

With a wicked grin, Jax pulls the bottle of maple syrup we used earlier from his back pocket—our playful innuendoes now heightened with newfound meaning. He drizzles a slow, sticky trail down my abdomen, his eyes never leaving mine.

"You've never known true decadence until you've tasted yourself with a hint of maple," he murmurs, his voice thick with desire. "Let me show you, Claire. Let me show you how good we can be together."

And as he brings his fingers to his lips, tasting me along with the amber syrup, the world around us melts away. I'm covered in sticky syrup, but I don't care as Jax's tongue licks it all off my heated skin.

I glance down and see him free himself from his pants. His heavy cock drops free, and I gasp when I see the liquid beading the tip. It's impossibly hard and straining toward me.

I stare, transfixed, at Jax's impressive length, my mouth going dry. I've never seen a man aroused before, and the sight sends a fresh gush of wetness between my thighs. He sees me looking and grins wickedly, wrapping a hand around himself and giving a slow, teasing stroke.

"Like what you see, sweetheart?"

I can only nod mutely, my brain short-circuiting as I watch his fist slide up and down his thick shaft. He's magnificent—all hard angles and coiled power, barely restrained. The hunger in his gaze threatens to devour me whole.

Jax settles his hips between my splayed thighs, the blunt head of his cock nudging insistently at my entrance. I tense instinctively, suddenly nervous. This is uncharted territory for me. But Jax cups my face, forcing me to meet his eyes.

"Relax, baby," he soothes, brushing a tender kiss across my lips. "I've got you. I'll make this so good for you, I promise."

Emboldened by his words, I let my legs fall

open further, welcoming him into the cradle of my body. Jax pushes forward, slowly, carefully, letting me adjust to the unfamiliar stretch and burn. It's intense, this feeling of fullness, of completion. Like a missing piece of myself I never knew was absent until this moment.

"God, you're so tight," Jax grits out, his face taut with restraint. "So perfect."

He hilts himself fully inside me with a low groan, and we both still, suspended in the gravity of our joining. I can feel every ridge and vein of him, pulsing deep within my core. It's overwhelming in the best possible way.

After a long, charged moment, Jax begins to move. He withdraws almost fully before surging back in, setting a steady, deep rhythm that has me seeing stars. Each thrust hits a spot inside me that I didn't even know existed, stoking the embers of my arousal into a raging inferno.

"That's it, sweetheart," he praises roughly as I arch to meet his strokes. "Take what you need."

I lose myself to the sensations—the delicious drag of his hardness, the dizzying spiral of pleasure building at the base of my spine. Nothing else exists outside this room, this bed, this man. Jax is my entire universe, the axis on which I spin.

He leans down to capture my lips in a searing

kiss, swallowing my increasingly desperate moans. One hand slides between our sweat-slicked bodies to find my aching center. He rubs tight, focused circles around the sensitive bundle of nerves, winding the coil of tension inside me tighter and tighter until it's unbearable.

"Let go, Claire," Jax commands, his voice rough with need. "Come for me, baby. I want to feel you fall apart."

His words are my undoing. With a keening cry, I shatter in his arms, my inner muscles clenching rhythmically around his pistoning length. Wave after wave of ecstasy crashes over me, whiting out my vision, stealing the air from my lungs. I clutch at Jax's shoulders, my nails digging red crescents into his skin as I ride out the aftershocks.

"That's it, sweetheart," he praises, never stopping the relentless pump of his hips. "God, you're exquisite when you come. I could watch you fall apart like this forever."

Jax picks up the pace, chasing his own release now. His thrusts become erratic, more forceful, hitting that secret spot inside me over and over until I'm teetering on the edge again, oversensitive and yearning.

"You're mine now, Claire," he growls possessively, his eyes flashing with primal hunger. "No other man will ever touch you like this. I'll make sure of it."

I can only moan in assent, too lost in sensation to form words. The knowledge that I'm his, completely and irrevocably, only heightens my arousal. I want to be owned by him, body and soul.

"Say it," Jax demands harshly, punctuating each word with a deep, grinding thrust. "Tell me you're mine."

"I'm yours," I gasp out, my back arching off the bed as he hits a particularly sensitive spot. "Only yours, Jax. Always."

My declaration seems to unleash something wild in him. With a guttural groan, he hoists my legs over his shoulders, the new angle allowing him to plunge even deeper. I cry out sharply, my body bowing under the onslaught of sensation.

"That's right, baby," he rasps. "Take all of me. I'm going to fill you up so good, ruin you for anyone else."

His filthy words and the relentless pounding of his cock catapult me to new heights. A second climax hits me without warning, even more intense than the first. I keen his name like a prayer as I convulse around him, stars exploding behind my tightly shut eyelids.

"Fuck, Claire," Jax snarls, his hips snapping

frantically now. "Your little virgin cunt is squeezing me so tight. Gonna make me come so hard..."

With a hoarse shout, he buries himself to the hilt and stills, his cock jerking inside me as he finds his own release. I can feel the hot rush of his seed painting my inner walls, marking me indelibly as his own.

The intimacy of it, the pure possession, sends me spiraling into a third shuddering climax, my body milking every last drop from Jax's pulsing length. We cling to each other as the aftershocks roll through us, chests heaving, sweat-slicked skin sliding deliciously.

After long moments, Jax carefully withdraws and collapses beside me, pulling me into the shelter of his arms. I tuck my face into the crook of his neck, breathing in the intoxicating scent of sex and spice and something uniquely him. My body still hums, nerve endings singing from the force of my release.

"That was..." I trail off, lacking the words to encompass the magnitude of what just transpired between us.

"Earth-shattering? Life-altering?" Jax supplies with a wicked grin, his fingertips tracing idle patterns on my hip.

I slap his chest playfully, a smile tugging at my

lips. "I was going to say intense. But yes, all of the above."

He chuckles, the sound a deep rumble beneath my cheek. "Oh, sweetheart. That was just the appetizer. Wait until you see what I have planned for the main course."

A delicious shiver races down my spine at the dark promise in his voice. If that was just the beginning, I can scarcely imagine what other decadent delights Jax has in store. The mere thought has desire unfurling anew in my still-quivering core.

As if reading my mind, Jax rolls me beneath him again, his weight a welcome anchor pinning me to the rumpled sheets. He nuzzles my neck, teeth grazing the sensitive skin of my throat.

"After dinner," he murmurs, his lips brushing the shell of my ear. "I'm going to spend all night feasting on you until you forget your own name."

I already can't wait.

four

. . .

Jax

I BUTTON UP MY SHIRT, watching Claire slide her dress back on with a satisfied smile. The sight of her glowing skin still sends a thrill through me, even as we prepare to head downstairs and play hosts once again. The kitchen staff has been bustling around, the aroma of roasted turkey and spiced pies wafting through the old inn.

As we enter the dining room, the long table is already set with gleaming silverware and elegant china. Guests begin to arrive, filling the space with jovial chatter and clinking glasses. I keep Claire close, my hand resting possessively on the small of her back as we make our rounds and greet everyone.

The dinner progresses smoothly, a delicious spread of traditional favorites and a few of my own gourmet twists. But as I savor a bite of stuffing, I notice a man leaning in close to Claire, his eyes roaming over her in a way that makes my blood boil. She laughs politely at something he says, but I can see the discomfort in the tightness of her smile.

Jealousy rears its ugly head inside me, a snarling beast clawing at my chest. I grip my fork tightly, knuckles turning white. How dare he look at her like that, as if she's his to covet? The urge to march over and rip him away from her consumes me.

Claire glances my way, her eyes widening slightly at the intensity etched on my face.

I want to whisk her away, to claim her as mine and mine alone. The thought of anyone else touching her, desiring her, fills me with a primal rage.

And then fucker puts his hands on her.

I stand abruptly, my chair scraping against the hardwood floor. The chatter in the room fades to a distant hum as jerk him up from his chair and thunder, "Get out!" at him.

I don't know who he is, and I frankly don't give a fuck because he's just crossed a line.

Everyone is staring at the scene I'm making, but again, I don't give a fuck. I tug Claire's hand, pulling her to a stand and then I lead her away from the curious gazes of our guests. She follows without hesitation, her trust in me evident in every step.

We weave through the inn's winding corridors, the air crackling with tension. My pulse races, the need to have her, to claim her, overwhelming all rational thought. I find a secluded alcove, hidden from prying eyes, and press her against the wall.

My hands frame her face, tilting her chin up to meet my burning gaze. "You're mine, Claire. *Mine*, and I'm not done with you yet," I growl, my voice rough with desire. "I'll never be done with you."

Claire's breath hitches, her lips parting in a silent gasp. I close the distance between us, capturing her mouth in a searing kiss. It's all tongues and teeth, a desperate clash of passion and possession. She melts into me, her hands fisting in my hair, pulling me closer.

I break the kiss, trailing my lips along her jawline, down the slender column of her neck. "Mine," I whisper desperately against her skin.

"Only mine. The thought of anyone else touching you drives me insane."

She arches into me, a soft moan escaping her. "Jax," she breathes, her voice thick with emotion. "I'm yours. Always."

My heart swells at her words, the intensity of my feelings for her nearly overwhelming. I claim her lips once more, pouring every ounce of my devotion, my hunger, into the kiss. She matches me, stroke for stroke, her own passion rising to meet mine.

I feel Claire's hands slide down my chest, her fingers deftly working at the buttons of my shirt. My breath catches as her nails graze my skin, leaving trails of fire in their wake. She pushes the fabric off my shoulders, her eyes dark with desire as she takes in the sight of me.

"My turn," she murmurs, a seductive smile playing at the corners of her mouth. She presses her palms against my chest, backing me up until I'm the one pinned against the wall. Her lips find my collarbone, teeth grazing the sensitive skin there, and I can't suppress the low groan that escapes me.

Claire's hands explore my body with a newfound boldness, each touch sending shockwaves of pleasure coursing through me. She's taking control, and it's intoxicating. I'm drowning in sensation, in the feel of her mouth on my skin, the press of her curves against me.

"Claire," I manage, my voice rough with need. "You're driving me crazy."

She looks up at me through her lashes, a coy smile on her kiss-swollen lips. "That's the idea," she whispers, her hands dipping lower, teasing along the waistband of my pants.

I capture her wrists, spinning us around so she's once again trapped between me and the wall. Our eyes lock, the air between us crackling with tension. In this moment, I know with startling clarity that this woman is my everything. The emotions swirling in her gaze, the way my heart races at her touch—it's something deeper, something that has taken root in my very soul.

I want to take care of her. I want to marry her. I want to put a baby in her belly like a man is supposed to do.

I crush my mouth to hers, the kiss a wordless promise of all the things I long to say. She responds with equal fervor, her fingers tangling in my hair, holding me close. We're lost in each other, the rest of the world fading away until there is only the two of us and this searing connection that grows stronger with every passing second.

And even though my cock is pressing insistently against the front of my pants, I make myself break the kiss.

We're both breathing heavily, and I rest my forehead against hers. "Claire," I murmur, my voice trembling with the force of my emotions. "Say you'll stay with me forever."

She stares at me, her eyes wide and luminous in the dim light. For a heart-stopping moment, I fear she doesn't feel the same, that I've misread the situation entirely. But then a slow, radiant smile spreads across her face, and she reaches up to cup my cheek.

"I want that too, Jax," she whispers, her thumb brushing over my skin in a featherlight caress. "I didn't expect this, didn't expect you, but now I can't imagine going back to my life without you in it."

Relief and joy surge through me, and I capture her hand, pressing a fervent kiss to her palm. "You've turned my world upside down, Claire Harper," I confess, my heart in my throat. "I've never felt this way about anyone before."

She leans in, her lips a hairsbreadth from mine. "I'm falling for you, Jax Donovan," she breathes, her words a sweet caress against my mouth. "Harder and faster than I ever thought possible."

Our lips meet in a kiss that seals our confessions, a promise of the future we'll build together. And then I have to have her.

I unbutton my pants, and my cock drops out, stiff and heavy. I hike Claire's dress up and push her panties to the side, groaning at the wetness that meets my fingers.

I slide my fingers through her slick heat, relishing the way her breath hitches. "Fuck, you're so wet for me," I groan against her neck. "Always so ready."

"Only for you," Claire gasps as I circle her sensitive nub. "I need you, Jax. Now."

I can't deny her, can't resist sinking into her welcoming warmth. I line myself up and thrust deep, swallowing her moan with a searing kiss. Her legs wrap around my hips as I start to move, my strokes hard and fast, driven by a primal need to claim her, to mark her as mine.

The alcove fills with the sounds of our passion—ragged breaths, desperate kisses, the erotic slap of skin on skin. Claire meets me thrust for thrust, her nails raking down my back, spurring me on.

"Harder," she pants. "Don't hold back. I want to feel you for days."

Her words unleash something wild in me, and I comply with a low growl, slamming into her with abandon. The pleasure builds rapidly, coiling tighter and tighter. I snake a hand between us, finding her clit, intent on bringing her with me over the edge.

"Come for me, Claire," I command hoarsely, rubbing rapid circles. "Let me feel you."

She shatters with a choked cry, her walls clamping down on me like a vice. I bury my face in her neck, muffling my shout as I follow her into bliss, emptying myself deep inside her.

We stay locked together, hearts racing, as we float down from the high. I pepper her face with soft kisses, marveling at the incredible woman in my arms.

"I love you," I murmur, the words spilling out unbidden. "I know it's fast, but I've never been more sure of anything in my life."

Claire's eyes shine with unshed tears. "I love you too, Jax. This is real, isn't it? What we have?"

I kiss her tenderly, pouring all my adoration into it. "It's the realest thing I've ever known. You're my everything now."

I hoist Claire into my arms and carry and carry her upstairs to my bedroom, relishing the feeling of her warm body nestled against my chest. The scent of her hair, the soft swell of her breasts pressed to me—it all feels like a dream I never want to wake from.

Gently laying her on the plush comforter, I drink in the sight of her spread out before me, cheeks flushed and eyes dark with desire. "You're so beautiful," I murmur reverently, trailing my fingertips along the silk of her inner thigh. "I want to worship every inch of you."

She shivers at my touch, back arching off the bed. "Please, Jax..." Her breathless plea is music to my ears.

I take my time undressing her, savoring each new expanse of creamy skin as it's revealed. Flicking open the front clasp of her lacy bra, I groan at the sight of her perfect breasts, rosy nipples already pebbled and begging for my mouth. I oblige, drawing one stiff peak between my lips to suck and nibble until she's writhing beneath me.

"You taste divine," I growl against her breast before moving lower, blazing a trail of hot, open-mouthed kisses down her quivering belly. Hooking my fingers in her panties, I tug the scrap of lace down her legs and toss it aside.

Claire watches me through heavy-lidded eyes, chest heaving with anticipation as I settle between her parted thighs. The first swipe of my tongue through her slick folds has her crying out, fingers twisting in my hair.

"Jax! Oh God..." She bucks against my face as I

feast on her sweet nectar, lapping and suckling her swollen clit. Sliding two fingers deep into her tight channel, I stroke that sensitive spot inside and feel her start to flutter around me.

"That's it, baby. Come for me," I coax, pumping faster, curling my fingers as I suckle her clit. With a sharp gasp, she shatters, thighs clamping around my head as she rides out the waves of her release.

I lap up every drop before crawling up her body to claim her mouth in a searing kiss. Claire moans at the taste of herself on my tongue, hands roaming greedily over my shoulders and back.

"I need you," she pants against my lips. "I need to feel you inside me. Please, Jax..."

"I've got you, sweetheart." Pushing to my knees, I free my aching cock and position myself at her entrance. With one smooth thrust, I bury myself to the hilt in her slick heat, a guttural groan escaping my throat at the exquisite feel of her gripping me like a vise.

"Fuck, you're so tight. So perfect," I rain kisses down on her face incoherently before I grip her hips and pull her flush against me as I start to move, long deep strokes that have her mewling and clutching at my forearms. Her silken walls hug my cock like they were made just for me, drawing me in deeper with every thrust.

"Harder, Jax," she gasps, nails digging deliciously into my skin. "I need you deeper."

A primal growl rumbles in my chest at her words. Hitching her leg higher on my hip, I comply with her breathy demands, snapping my hips faster, harder, the force of my thrusts rocking the headboard against the wall. Claire arches beneath me, the new angle letting me hit that sweet spot inside her with every stroke. Her cries of pleasure fill the room, spurring me on, driving me closer to the edge.

"Touch yourself for me, Claire," I grit out, my eyes locked on hers, dark with lust and need. "I want to feel you come on my cock."

Holding my heated gaze, she obeys, sliding a hand between our sweat-slicked bodies to circle her swollen clit. I can feel the flutter of her walls as she works herself closer to climax, her breath coming in short, sharp pants.

"That's it, baby," I encourage roughly, fighting the urge to let go, determined to bring her over first. "Come for me. Let me feel you."

With a keening cry, Claire shatters in my arms, her body going taut as she pulses and clenches around my thrusting cock. The rippling vice of her sex is my undoing, and with a hoarse shout, I follow her over the precipice, spilling myself deep inside her welcoming heat.

I collapse on top of her, my face buried in the crook of her neck as we struggle to catch our breath. Claire's fingers card gently through my sweat-dampened hair, and I press a tender kiss to her racing pulse.

"I love you," I murmur against her skin, the words a sacred vow. "I'm never letting you go."

She cups my face in her hands, bringing my mouth to hers for a slow, sweet kiss that makes my heart ache with the depth of my feelings for her.

"I love you too, Jax," she whispers, her eyes shimmering with emotion.

My chest tightens at her words. This beautiful creature loves me...

I drop feather-light kisses across Claire's face as we catch our breath, our hearts beating in sync. "This is the best Thanksgiving I've ever had," I murmur against her soft skin, inhaling her intoxicating scent. "You've made it unforgettable in every way."

A sultry smile curves her kiss-swollen lips. "Mmm, I don't think I've ever been more...stuffed," she smiles, trailing a finger down my chest.

My cock twitches at her words, already stirring to life again. "Is that so?" I nip playfully at her earlobe. "Well, far be it from me to leave you unsatisfied on Thanksgiving."

Rolling her beneath me, I kiss a searing path down her neck to her breasts, lavishing attention on the sensitive peaks until she's arching off the bed. "Jax, please..." she keens, fingers tangling in my hair.

"Please what, sweet Claire?" I rasp, my hand skimming down her trembling body to tease her slick folds. "Tell me what you need."

"You," she gasps as I circle her swollen clit. "I need you. I'll always need you."

Surging up, I claim her mouth in a deep, drugging kiss, our tongues tangling feverishly. She wraps her legs around my hips, urging me closer. The head of my cock nudges her entrance and I pause, drinking in the sight of her flushed and wanton beneath me.

"I'm going to fill you up, Claire," I promise darkly. "Stuff you so full of my cum. Put my baby in this sweet belly." I stroke reverent fingers over her flat stomach, imagining it growing round and ripe with my child.

Claire's breath hitches, her eyes flaring with primal heat. "Yes," she moans, tilting her hips in blatant invitation. "Jax, please. I want that, want you. Now and always."

With a low growl, I surge forward, sheathing myself to the hilt in her welcoming body. We both cry out at the exquisite sensation, so deeply joined. I start to move, rolling my hips in a steady rhythm that soon has her clutching at my shoulders, my name a litany on her lips.

"Harder," she pants, scoring my back with her nails. "Stuff me with your cum, Jax."

My control shatters. Hoisting her leg higher on my hip, I pound into her, the force of my thrusts rocking the bed. The wet slap of flesh, our harsh breaths and moans of pleasure fill the room. Tension coils tighter and tighter at the base of my spine as I chase my release.

"Come with me, Claire," I command hoarsely, grinding against her clit. "Milk my cock, let me feel you come undone."

Her walls clench around me in fluttering pulses as she cries out, her climax crashing over her. The rapturous sight of her pleasure, the satin heat rippling along my shaft, sends me hurtling into ecstasy. With a guttural shout, I bury myself to the hilt and erupt, painting her womb with thick ropes of my seed.

I collapse on top of her, both of us gasping for breath, sweat-slicked skin sliding deliciously. Claire's fingers delve into my hair, scratching lightly at my scalp as I press open-mouthed kisses to her neck, her jaw, the corner of her lush mouth.

"I love you," I rasp, still buried deep within her, reluctant to ever withdraw from her sweet heat. "I want to build a life with you, Claire. Grow old with you. Keep you barefoot and pregnant."

She cups my face, her eyes bright with unshed tears. "I want that too, Jax. More than I've ever wanted anything, but it's all so fast, it's kind of scary."

I roll to the side, gathering her close, tangling our limbs together until we're a knot of sated flesh and racing hearts. "You never have to be scared with me," I vow solemnly, brushing my lips against her brow. "I'll always keep you safe. Cherish you. Love you until my very last breath."

We make love twice more that night, soft and slow, savoring each touch, each whispered endearment. When sleep finally claims us, it's with Claire's head pillowed on my chest, our fingers entwined over my steadily beating heart.

I know I'll never let her go, this enchanting woman who's captured me so completely. My last thought before slipping into dreams is of the shining future stretching out before us, full of laughter and love and the pitter-patter of tiny feet.

I'll always keep her stuffed.

epilogue

. . .

Five years later

Claire

THE AROMA of simmering marinara sauce and bubbling mozzarella fills the kitchen as I expertly twirl pizza dough, flour dusting my hands and apron. Jax stands beside me, chopping fresh basil and oregano from the herb garden just outside. His muscular arms flex with each slice of the knife, a sight I never tire of even after five years of marriage.

"Mommy, mommy! Look what I drew!" Our four-year-old twins, Liam and Noah, come barreling into the kitchen, crayon masterpieces flapping in their little hands. Their exuberant footsteps patter across the tile, narrowly avoiding Jax as he sidesteps them with the ease of a seasoned dad-chef.

"Those look amazing, my little Picassos!" I exclaim, setting the dough aside to admire their colorful scribbles of our family. "Why don't you go put those on the fridge while Daddy and I finish making pizza?"

As they scamper off, Jax slides behind me, arms encircling my waist, his lips grazing the sensitive spot just below my ear. "I don't know how you do it all," he murmurs, admiration lacing his husky voice. "Keeping up with the kids, the blog, the brand deals. You're Super Mom."

I lean back into his solid warmth, savoring his closeness amidst the beautiful chaos of our life. The meteoric rise of our cooking brand still feels surreal at times—the successful blog, Jax's acclaimed restaurant at the inn, the cookbook deals and TV appearances. But this, right here, is what grounds me. Our love, our family, creating something together in the heart of our home.

"I couldn't do any of it without my partner in everything," I reply, turning in his arms to press a soft kiss to his lips, tasting the faint remnants of the wine he used for the sauce. "Especially on days like today."

Jax's hands settle on my hips as he grins down at me, eyes crinkling with mirth. "Well, running a restaurant does come with a few perks. Like an endless supply of gourmet pizza ingredients for family dinner night."

Laughter bubbles up my throat, mingling with the kids' gleeful shrieks from the living room and the mouthwatering scent of browning crust in the oven. This beautiful life we've built, brick by brick, is more than I could have imagined all those years ago when a charming innkeeper first swept me off my feet.

We enjoy dinner and a children's movie as a family, and my heart swells at the gently way Jax plays with our sons, the joy evident in his eyes.

The boys are still playing, though it's evident they're getting sleepy as I clean up in the kitchen with Jax has a cooking competition with the boys with their play kitchen and food.

"Bedtime!" I finally call out, gently separating from Jax's embrace as our rambunctious twins reluctantly bid farewell to their daddy-son cooking competition. The twinkle in their eyes mirrors their father's, and I can't help but smile at the thought of the delicious chaos tomorrow will bring.

As I tuck them in, I'm struck by the warmth in my chest, the knowledge that our crazy, messy, food-fueled life is exactly what my heart has always yearned for. And as I close the door to their room, I can't help but linger, my senses filled with the aroma of love, laughter, and the promise of more to come.

Back in the kitchen, Jax is busy arranging putting away the dishes. He turns as he senses my presence, his eyes raking over me with a heat that hasn't dulled in the slightest. "Clean-up is almost finished." His hungry gaze rakes over me, and I shiver.

Five years, and the spark between us hasn't dulled in the slightest. In fact, it's only grown stronger.

I can't help but grin, feeling a shiver of anticipation traipsing down my spine. "And what do you have in mind for dessert, Chef Donovan?" I ask, adopting a playful lilt to my voice.

He quirks an eyebrow, a slow, sexy smirk curving his lips. "Well, Mrs. Donovan, I was thinking of a little stuffing." His eyes darken, and the air between us crackles with the same electricity I've felt since the moment we met.

Without another word, I step into his arms, my body molding to his as if we've been doing this dance for lifetimes. His hands slide down my hips, fingers dancing along the curve of my thighs, sending goosebumps prickling along my skin. I gasp, his name catching in my throat as his lips brush against my neck, then down, trailing a trail of fire that leaves me breathless.

"Jax," I moan, my legs threatening to give out beneath me. He chuckles, his hand finding my thigh, lifting me effortlessly onto the marble countertop.

His hand brushes my sex, and his breath hitches at the wetness he finds.

"Eager, are we?" he asks, his voice a deep rumble that settles in the pit of my stomach. I blush, but I can't find it in me to deny the truth. His fingers graze my cheek , tucking a stray curl behind my ear. "Lucky for you, I've got something special in mind for my very naughty wife," he whispers, his voice low and sultry.

I shudder as he slowly unbuttons my blouse, his fingers grazing the swell of my breasts. The cool marble countertop contrasts deliciously with the heat of Jax's body pressing against mine.

"You're so beautiful," he murmurs reverently, eyes drinking me in like a man parched. "I'll never get enough of you, Claire."

His mouth claims mine in a searing kiss,

tongues tangling, breath mingling. I moan into him, fingers raking through his thick hair, pulling him impossibly closer. He groans, hips rocking into me, his hardness straining against his jeans.

With deft fingers, Jax unclasps my bra, freeing my aching breasts. He lavishes them with attention, sucking one pebbled nipple into the wet heat of his mouth while his hand kneads the other. Pleasure zings through me, coiling tighter and tighter in my core.

"Jax, please," I whimper, writhing beneath his touch, desperate for more.

He smirks against my skin, trailing open-mouthed kisses down the valley of my breasts, over the quivering plane of my stomach. Hooking his fingers in my waistband, he drags my leggings and lace panties down my legs in one smooth motion.

I'm bared before him, glistening and wanting. His heated gaze rakes over me possessively.

"Mine," he growls. "All mine."

Then his head dips between my thighs and I'm lost. His tongue traces my slick folds, circling my clit, stoking the flames higher. My head falls back, a cry torn from my throat as two fingers sink deep inside me, curling just right.

"You taste divine," Jax rasps, lapping and sucking, driving me to the brink. "Come for me, sweetheart. I want to feel you."

With a final flick of his tongue, I shatter, muscles clenching rhythmically around his fingers as ecstasy crashes over me in waves. He works me through it, prolonging the bliss, until I'm boneless and sated.

Jax kisses his way back up my body, pausing to lavish my breasts again. I fumble with his belt, freeing his impressive length, stroking him root to tip. He hisses, hips bucking into my touch.

"I need to be inside you," he pants, lining himself up. With a smooth thrust, he sheathes himself to the hilt, stretching and filling me so perfectly. We both groan at the exquisite sensation.

He sets a deep, rolling rhythm, grinding against my clit with every stroke. I wrap my legs high around his waist, fingernails digging into his back, urging him deeper. Our bodies move as one, slick with sweat, the air thick with our mingled moans and sighs.

"God, Claire," Jax grunts, his thrusts growing more erratic as he chases his release. "You feel incredible. So tight, so perfect."

I clench around him purposefully and he swears, hips snapping forward harder. The coil in my core winds tighter, pleasure sparking through my veins like electricity. I'm so close, teetering on the knife's edge.

"Jax, I'm going to...I need..." I babble incoherently, lost to the intensity of the sensations consuming me.

"That's it, baby," he encourages, one hand snaking between us to rub firm circles over my swollen nub. "Let go for me. I've got you."

His words are my undoing. I come undone with a silent scream, my walls fluttering wildly around his plunging length. Jax follows me over with a hoarse shout of my name, spilling deep inside me as he finds his own release.

We cling to each other as the aftershocks fade, hearts pounding, chests heaving. Jax peppers tender kisses across my face, brushing damp tendrils of hair from my forehead.

"I love you," he murmurs, and the pure adoration shining in his eyes steals my breath. "More than anything."

"I love you too," I whisper back fiercely, cupping his face in my hands. "Forever and always."

He smiles softly, nuzzling into my touch. Carefully, he lifts me into his arms and carries me to our bedroom. We make love twice more, slow and sweet, reaffirming our devotion with every caress, every breathless sigh.

Afterward, we lay tangled together, limbs entwined, basking in the afterglow. As I drift off to sleep, secure in Jax's embrace, I'm filled with a bone-deep contentment.

This is where I belong. This is my happily ever after. And I wouldn't trade a single moment of our messy, beautiful, food-filled life together for anything in the world.

Want a free book from Emma Bray? Go to www.authoremmabray.com.

Keep reading for an excerpt from Rocky Christmas.

Rocky

I take a sip of my club soda as I watch the boxing match on the big screen.

While I'd love to have a beer, that's not what I'm here for. When I'm scheduled to fight in a match, I go through a grueling process of abstinence. I watch my diet. No processed or refined foods. Only healthy, whole foods. No alcohol. No fucking—not that there's been any fucking for me for years. I have two hands to sate my needs with, but I even abstain from self-gratification before a match.

My trainers insist that a strict diet with no drugs of any kind, including alcohol, and no sex helps build up the testosterone needed to really channel a good fight. I don't know how much I believe all that shit, but I do know I want to make sure my body is a well-honed machine when fight time comes around, so I follow their advice.

I'm not much for heavy drink anyway. I prefer to keep a clear head about myself, but a good beer is hard to beat every now and then. After this match, I'll have me one, I silently promise myself as I take another swig of the soda.

"Ooh, that's gotta hurt," the guy to my right says, his eyes glued to the screen. I look back up at the TV as Riker delivers a right hook to his opponent.

I grunt in agreement. My brother sure knows his stuff when it comes to boxing.

I'm glad I was able to talk him into taking it up instead of watching him waste away up on the top of that mountain he lives on. He's only in his early thirties—like me—but he went into the military when we were younger—unlike me. He's never told me what happened over there. All I know is that he came back a different man. He won't talk to me. He won't talk to reporters. Hell, he won't talk to anyone.

Before I turned him on to boxing, he used to just sit up in his house secluded away from everyone, brooding and doing fuck who knows what.

He's got a lot of rage in him. Anyone can tell that by watching him box. You don't box the way he does without having something to work out. At least he has an outlet to channel his frustration into.

I like a good boxing match too, but my strengths lie in MMA. I like the variety. I like the combativeness of it, and while I don't have the aggression and internal turmoil my brother does, I have a passion for the sport.

Riker KO's his opponent a minute later, and pride fills my chest for my brother. The ref holds Riker's hand up, declaring him the champion of the match. My brother accepts the applause, but he doesn't look jubilant like most victors of a fight do. He's just as stoic as usual, with the same grim, no-nonsense expression he's worn since he came back from overseas.

I plop down some money on the bar and stand.

Now that the match is over, I can go home and rest up for my own match.

I'm mentally calculating the time difference between my brother and me so that I can figure out when to give him a call to congratulate him on his latest win when I turn around and stop dead in my tracks.

My eyes light on a mass of fiery red hair that tumbles down a slender back. Those red locks almost touch the top of the woman's ass, and I stare at them mesmerized. The locks are full and wild, curling out every which way. I've never been the kind of guy who gets off on hair, but this woman's hair is fucking beautiful. My fingers twitch at my sides. I have the sudden urge to spear my hands into that hair and see if it feels as soft and silky as it looks.

The curls bounce as the girl tips her head back and laughs before she hops off the barstool beside her grinning friend, a brunette who I hardly notice out of the corner of my eyes because my gaze is pinned on the pretty little redhead.

She can't be much more than five feet tall, and when she looks in my direction, my chest tightens like I've been punched in the gut when I look into the prettiest pair of green eyes I've ever seen.

They're big and innocent-looking and framed by thick, dark lashes.

I know fucking is on my list of prohibited activities, but I'd break every rule in the book for a chance to get my dick wet by this pretty little redhead, but it's not even about that. I'm not just looking at her in lust, though I'd be lying if I said I'm not practically salivating at the thought of burying myself inside what I already know is going to be the tightest little pussy in the world.

No, it's more than that. I feel something I've never felt before surge inside me when I look at her. I don't just want to stick my dick inside her. I want to wrap her up in my arms and hold her close to me forever. I want to crawl inside her head and learn everything there is to know about her.

I blink when I realize I would be happy just to talk to her. I want to get to know her. There's something about her.

I know that if I ever did get inside her, there's no way I'd ever be able to let her go.

My head should be in the game. I should be mentally prepping myself for my fight tomorrow. A lot of big players have bet money on me. I know that. I don't want to let them down. I don't want to let myself down.

But right now, the only thing I can think about

is the pretty little redhead across the bar and finding out what her name is.

I take another sip of my club soda before I plop it back down on the bar. I grimace. Fuck, I wish that was a beer.

I might can abstain from alcohol for the sake of the match, but there's no way I'm going to leave this bar without finding out who this tiny angel is.

Holly

Cara's eyes widen as they focus on something behind me.

My laugh dies off, and I turn, my own eyes widening when I see what she sees.

The biggest, burliest man I've ever seen in my entire life is stalking over toward us. A thick, dark brown beard adorns the bottom half of his face. His shirt is molded to the ridges of muscles straining against his T-shirt like it's all the fabric can do to contain all that manliness.

Even though it's winter in Denver, this man is

wearing short sleeves like he laughs in the face of the cold weather. Tats decorate his arms.

He's a powerhouse of masculinity.

Good lord, what does this man do? Weight-lift cars?

All that muscle must be more than enough to protect him against winter's chill, but I'm wrapped up in a turtleneck sweater. I'm also wearing a big, fluffy coat too. I stay cold all the time, but this man…something tells me that his big body is like a furnace.

I'm proved correct when he finally stops right in front of me—so close to me that there's scarcely an inch left between our bodies. I tip my head up to look at the giant towering over me. I'm barely five foot two, so I'm short even compared to the average person, but this guy is way above average. He has to be well over six feet tall, making me appear even teenier and tinier than usual.

His eyes are a deep brown, like the finest chocolate.

They bore down into me in a way that sends all the blood rushing to my cheeks.

His eyes have taken mine captive. I couldn't look away from them if I tried.

I vaguely register Cara murmuring something, but I can't make out what she's saying over the roaring in my ears. It's like this man has caused everything around me to dim.

The man's eyes rove over my face as if he's trying to commit all of it to memory before one of his giant hands reach out to gently touch my hair.

His lips part slightly, and my breath hitches.

"What's your name, sweetheart?" His voice is like a big rumble of thunder, and it sends little shock waves rolling through me.

"Holly." I don't even contemplate not answering him because I'm suddenly dying to know who he is too.

I don't even have to prompt him for his own name.

"Holly," he tastes my name on his lips and nods his head in approval.

My blush deepens, pleasure unfurling deep in my belly at the look of approval on his face.

"I'm Rocky," that deep voice rumbles again.

"Rocky," I repeat his name like he did mine, and his eyes close for a moment as if he's savoring the sound of it.

"Say it again," he rumbles.

My cheeks flame even brighter, but I give him what he wants.

"Rocky."

A shudder goes through his big frame. "I've

Stuffed

never liked the sound of my name so much," he growls before he pins me in his intense gaze again.

He takes a deep breath before he says, his eyes never leaving mine, "I'm not good with subterfuge, Holly. I'm not one of those guys who's going to dance around what he wants and ease into it. I see what I want, and I go after ut."

My heart beats against my ribcage as the intensity in his eyes deepens.

"When I saw you across the room just now…" He shakes his big head before he continues. "I don't know what happened, but fuck, I want you."

My breath catches.

He rushes on, "I know I'm coming on strong, and I don't want to freak you out, but I don't see any point in beating around the bush. I'm going to make you mine."

The way he says *mine* comes out as a growl, and my heart flutters at the possessive way he's looking at me—like I already belong to him.

This is crazy. I don't know anything about this guy, and I've never wanted to belong to someone before. A monologue like this coming from any other man would undoubtedly infuriate me. It would come off as cocky and arrogant, but it doesn't come off that way with this man.

I get the sense that this isn't just some line he uses, that he's speaking from his soul.

And I'm loving the sound of him making me *his*.

It calls to me on a primal level. Even though he's the biggest, scariest-looking man I've ever seen, I also somehow feel completely safe in his presence—like nothing could ever hurt me.

When I don't speak, he runs a hand through his hair, a look of regret and self-loathing on his face.

"Fuck, I've just scared the shit out of you."

Frustration pours off him. He looks like he wishes he could beat himself up.

I instinctively want to soothe him. I lay a hand on his big arm, my fingers trembling atop his muscles.

He instantly stills, his eyes flicking up to mine and his chest heaving up and down at my touch. His nostrils flare, but I keep my hand on his arm. I feel like I'm calming a big beast. It both humbles me and empowers me at the same time. Seeing what I do to him almost makes me dizzy.

"You haven't scared me." I shake my head. "It's just…no one has ever said these things to me before."

He visibly relaxes before he covers my hand with his own. "Let me get to know you." His voice is gruff, and it scrapes over me like sandpaper. "We can go as slow as you want. I just want to spend some time with you, get to know you."

He fingers my hair again, a look of wonder in his eyes. "You're the most beautiful little thing I've ever seen," he murmurs.

My heart races again. He's looking at me like I'm the most precious thing he's ever seen. No one has ever looked at me this way before.

As the senator's daughter, I haven't dated much. I've always been so cautious. I've always had to be careful of who I'm seeing with so it doesn't look bad on my father or his career. I've never dated anyone who wasn't vetted and approved by him. My whole life has been planned out around my dad's career.

I've been complacent. I've never done anything just for me in all of my twenty-one years.

As Rocky's eyes bore down into mine, I realize that I'm tired of living that way. I want to do something for me.

I want Rocky. He's going to be that something just for me.

I'm tired of only dating the guys my dad sets me up with because their connections will further his career. I want to be with someone who wants me just for *me* and not what a connection with my father can do for them.

Rocky doesn't have a clue who I am. That much is obvious.

And that's why I'm not going to tell him my last name. I don't want to ruin this before it ever even begins.

My pulse races as I do the first thing I've ever done just for myself. "I want to get to know you, too."

Get Rocky Christmas here: Rocky Christmas.